SOLEIL'S
JOURNEY HOME

To: Emma

Happy Trail

Lois Thelderby

SOLEIL'S JOURNEY HOME

Written by
Lisa Holderby

Illustrations by
Sheila Walker

This book is dedicated to the memory
of my mother, Irma Holderby, who passed
away in 2010. Mother, thank you for your gift
of unconditional love, for giving me the
opportunity of living my dream, and for
encouraging me to share my story with others.

Introduction

Soleil's Journey Home is mostly a book of fiction and the sequel to *Soleil, A Mustang's Story*. The areas mentioned throughout this story are landmarks, towns, and places out West, close to the area where Soleil was captured in 2005. The map was supplied by The Bureau of Land Management's Wild Horse and Burro Program, with markings showing where Soleil was captured. A portion of the proceeds of this book will be donated to support the organizations that give their time, talent, and teamwork to help these wonderful horses. I have never had a horse exhibit as much love and loyalty as Soleil. I hope this book will inspire others to adopt and enjoy their life with a mustang.

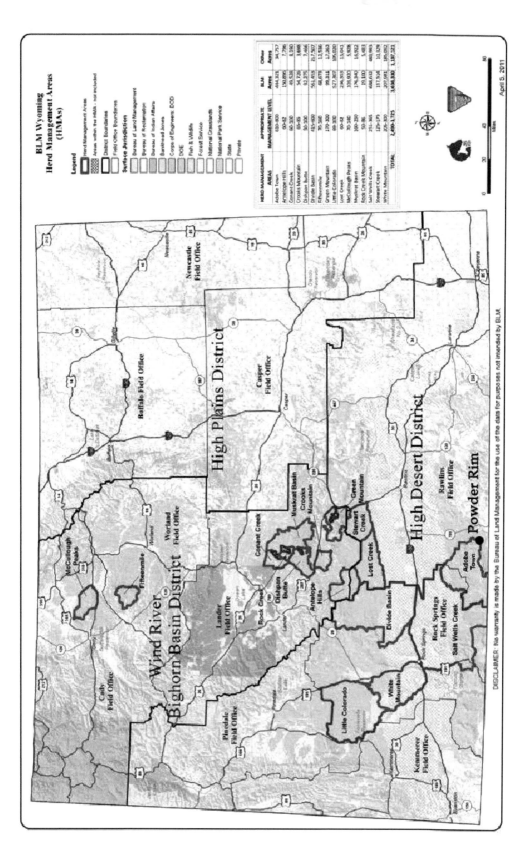

BLM Wyoming
Herd Management Areas
(HMAs)

Legend

Herd Management Areas
Areas within the HMAs - not included
District Boundaries
Field Office Boundaries

Surface Jurisdiction

Bureau of Land Management
Bureau of Reclamation
Bureau of Indian Affairs
Barehead Areas
Corps of Engineers: DOS
DOE
Fish & Wildlife
Forest Service
National Grasslands
National Parks Service
State
Private

HERD MANAGEMENT AREAS	APPROPRIATE MANAGEMENT LEVEL	BLM Acres	Other Acres
Adobe Town	610-800	444,321	34,757
Antelope Hills	60-82	130,895	7,796
Conant Creek	60-100	49,536	8,160
Crooks Mountain	65-85	54,726	3,666
Dishpan Butte	50-100	62,395	9,466
Divide Basin	415-600	561,455	217,507
Fifteenmile	70-160	68,679	13,586
Green Mountain	170-300	99,314	17,263
Little Colorado	69-100	527,307	106,630
Lost Creek	60-82	296,959	15,041
McCullough Peaks	70-140	108,000	5,838
Muskrat Basin	160-250	176,340	16,592
Rock Creek Mountain	50-86	19,100	5,483
Salt Wells Creek	251-365	608,610	603,993
Stewart Creek	125-175	157,504	10,329
White Mountain	205-300	207,081	185,002
TOTAL:	2,499-1725	3,694,830	1,187,321

Buffalo Field Office

Newcastle Field Office

High Plains District

Casper Field Office

Worland Field Office

Wind River
Bighorn Basin District

McCullough Peaks

Fifteenmile

Cody Field Office

Lander Field Office

Rock Creek

Dishpan Butte

Muskrat Basin
Conant Creek
Crooks Mountain

Green Mountain
Stewart Creek

Antelope Hills

Lost Creek

High Desert District

Divide Basin

Rawlins Field Office

Pinedale Field Office

Little Colorado

White Mountain

Rock Springs Field Office

Salt Wells Creek

Adobe Town

Powder Rim

Kemmerer Field Office

DISCLAIMER: No warranty is made by the Bureau of Land Management for the use of the data for purposes not intended by BLM.

April 5, 2011

0   20   40   80
Miles

*"Don't take for granted the things closest
to your heart. Cling to them as you would
your life, for without them, life is meaningless."*

From Nancye Simms
A Creed to Live By

Contents

Chapter One

Remembering the Herd

Wind funneled down the mountain, and the air smelled of sagebrush and fresh evergreens. The mountaintops were rocky and bare of trees. Soleil—the once wild mustang that had been adopted by Elizabeth nearly three years ago—knew she was close to her old home in the Rocky Mountains. She stood facing west, nose in the air, quivering to the familiar smells that filled her senses. *I know where I am*, she thought. *I can smell the other horses.* Soleil circled in her corral, tossing her head in frustration at being left here alone by Elizabeth. A new person had been riding her, and Soleil had never accepted another rider. Elizabeth was the only person who had ever ridden her. Soleil disliked the weight of the big man who had been riding her since she arrived at the ranch, and she had tried to buck him off at first. She was used to Elizabeth's ways and her feel in the saddle. The big man worked her hard. He introduced her to cattle and other new things she wasn't used to seeing or doing. *Someone let me loose*, she neighed sadly.

Still pacing in circles, she knew she had once roamed with the wild herd close to where she was now. The smells and sounds reminded her of when she was a foal and of the day she ran in the meadow with her mother—the day she was captured. This evening was crisp and cool, just like the day she had lost her horse family. *Where did you go?* Soleil nickered, half expecting a familiar neigh back. But a neigh did not sound back. Soleil felt abandoned. She stopped pacing and looked one more time to the west. Feeling defeated, she lay down alone in the middle of the corral. She was not allowed to pasture with the other horses at the ranch. *Why did Elizabeth leave me here?* She nickered one more time toward the other horses at the ranch.

* * * * *

Several miles away, another horse traveled a well-worn path that led to a small canyon. Salt Wells Creek ran through the mountains here, and the creek was a source of water for the wild horses. The old mare leading the herd knew the canyon would offer a safe place for the horses to bed down until morning. The trail crossed over to Pine Butte, an area where she had lived for many years. Cold water flowed down the mountains, and the canyon walls would be cool this warm night. During the day the sun heated the canyon's red walls, and at night the water cooled the small cove. The old mare knew where to bring the herd at night. The herd—led by a young stallion, a palomino—had grown smaller over the last few years. A number of the younger foals had not survived the food shortage of the previous winter. The remaining yearlings had been captured during the spring roundup by the Bureau of Land Management.

For many years, the old mare had led the herd to the safety of this remote canyon. The hidden cove had kept them safe from many predators, including man. The old mare had learned how to survive and had avoided being captured.

Climbing slowly up the narrow path, the horses followed the old mare to the cold water that ran through the canyon. Stopping in the creek, she looked over to make sure the herd had made it in and then lowered her head to drink the fresh water.

The palomino stallion watched from a distance while the other horses lowered their mouths into the stream. He would be the last to drink the water. He would have to make sure the herd was safe before drinking. The horses had traveled many miles for water, and this was a normal routine in the summer. After the herd had watered, the stallion finally bent down to drink.

The sun was sinking deeper with the end of dusk, capturing the pink colors that faded off the rugged mountains and setting for the day. The old mare turned and lay down; it had been a long journey. The stallion would stand watch while she slept. The night was quiet except for a lone coyote that echoed its eerie sound in the distance. The old mare closed her eyes and slept.

Hours later, the light of dawn stirred her.

She listened for other sounds while rising to her feet. Her movement would wake the other horses. Wyoming was dry this time of year. This would be their last watering hole before reaching the high meadows at Powder Rim. They would have to travel several more miles to the grassy plains. The stallion watched the old mare head down the canyon, his blond mane blowing in the wind.

Moving swiftly, the horses jumped over gullies and sagebrush. Carefully judging the steep terrain, the old mare cautiously stepped down the rugged trail. In this country only the strong survived. Soon the fall snows would come and cover the meadows and grassland, which would stay frozen until spring. Down the trail the horses traveled, the old mare leading the herd down winding paths. They picked up speed on the wider sections. The meadows were just around the bend.

Suddenly, the old mare stopped. She lifted her nose and smelled the air. Below in the meadow stood the band of horses that belonged to the old bay stallion. The two stallions had fought before, and the older and more experienced big bay had taken most of the younger stallion's herd.

The palomino stallion was still scarred from their last encounter, fighting fiercely over the mares. He galloped past the old mare toward the older bay stallion. Their deep screams echoed off the mountains and into the valley. The older stallion reared, accepting the challenge of the younger stallion. The palomino charged aggressively at the bay horse.

The old mare watched quietly. She could see that the big bay stallion had deep wounds from a previous fight. His rear leg was injured. This time of year was breeding time when the younger horses were always challenging the herd stallions. The big bay met the palomino's challenge with bared teeth, striking the younger stallion with great force. The two horses stood on hind quarters for an instant, biting and striking with their front legs. The big bay was pushed back. With an injured leg, he could not hold ground to the younger stallion. The palomino attacked harder, gaining leverage on the older horse and striking the wounded leg out of instinct. The big bay fell backward. The fight was over in minutes.

The land was hard and cruel but that was the way of the wild for the horses.

The old mare watched from a distance; she

would gather up the big bay stallion's band so it would join hers. There were a few scraps rising among the horses until the old mare led them to the sweet grass in the meadow. The bay stallion hobbled off and left the safety of the group; he looked back at his herd one last time before limping into the forest. The horses quieted, and the young palomino reared and pawed the air. The young stallion had regained the herd so he was the victor this time. Galloping toward the new herd, he turned and looked one last time for the bay but it had already disappeared into the forest.

* * * * *

At the ranch, it was dawn. Soleil stood up and listened, shaking herself. She was growing tired of staying in the small pasture. *Someone let me out,* she neighed loudly. The sounds and smells had stirred old feelings of running free, things she hadn't remembered for a long time. *She was home, the place where she was born . . . and had been captured.*

Chapter Two

The Circle T

The plane made its final descent into the small airport at Rock Canyon, Wyoming. With sleepy eyes, Emily looked out the window at the mountaintops. "Elizabeth, we're here?" she sighed.

Elizabeth smiled and answered, "Yes, we're here. Honey, see the runway?" Emily rubbed her eyes, trying to wake up. "Do you think Soleil has made it yet?" she asked groggily from her nap.

Elizabeth patted her arm. "Emily, Soleil has been here for two weeks, silly, wake up." Finally awake, Emily turned and looked at Elizabeth. "Wow, I forgot. Look how big the mountains look from here!"

Elizabeth looked out the window and smiled. Instantly she said, "Yes, and that's where we'll be going in a couple days, into those big old mountains!" Elizabeth was worried about the trip and hoped she had made the right decision by bringing Soleil back to where she was born and had been captured. Soleil was well trained but having a group of wild horses running by could cause any horse to get excited and take off. She glanced over at Emily, who was still looking out the window, and smiled.

Gliding above the runway, the plane touched down smoothly. Elizabeth looked at her watch. "We're right on time, Emily!" Both were excited to be in Wyoming after all of their preparations for the trip. Elizabeth was weary from packing and traveling but managed to rally once they landed. She couldn't believe she was finally out west after planning the trip for over a year. She was also excited to meet the reporter again, who was doing the follow-up article on the wild mustangs. The last article was very much talked about, and more people were interested in the horses. This time the reporter would be doing a follow-up article about Elizabeth bringing Soleil, the once wild mustang, back to Powder Rim, the place she was captured by the Bureau of Land Management.

The plane taxied down the runway. Elizabeth quickly grabbed their carry-on bags and ushered Emily off the plane to beat the rush out of town. They had to stop at an outdoor supplies store to get all the gear they still needed for the week's campout in the mountains. Then they'd go right to the ranch.

The two stepped off the plane to a warm summer day. Wyoming was stunning this time of year with its huge mountains surrounding the small airport.

"I may not want to go back home. It's so beautiful here," Emily laughed.

"Emily, please take the bags while I find the rental car place," Elizabeth said, not wanting to waste any time. She had spoken yesterday to Bud McClain, the horseman who had been training Soleil since the horse had arrived at the Circle T Ranch a couple of weeks ago. Bud was an "as good as it gets" horse trainer at the ranch. He had worked the ranch since he was a boy. The Circle T was a cattle ranch that had been passed down to three generations of McClains. Anxious to see Soleil and also to see how her training was going, Elizabeth hurried to get the rental car. Emily gathered their bags as Elizabeth pulled up in the SUV.

Helping Emily with the bags, Elizabeth filled the back of the van with their luggage.

"Gee, Elizabeth, we sure do need a lot of stuff for one trip!" Emily said.

Perspiration beaded off Elizabeth's forehead as she organized the back of the van. "Yes, but you won't think so if we need any of it and haven't reached one of the checkpoints where we can buy more supplies. Besides, we'll still need more gear for the trip. Hop in and plug the address of the ranch into the GPS system."

"Wow, this is exciting, Liz. All of us on a camping trip to see the wild horses." Emily beamed with excitement. "Soleil will be so happy to see her old home, and I'll get to pick out my own mustang . . . yeah! Do you think Soleil's mother and father were captured, too?" Emily asked.

"Nobody's going anywhere, young lady, until you get the address in the GPS," Elizabeth answered with a laugh. Emily put her hand over her mouth. In her excitement she had forgotten to put the address of the ranch into the GPS. She hurried and typed in the ranch address for Elizabeth.

Circle T Ranch was west of Rock Springs,

about an hour's drive. Elizabeth wanted to get to the ranch before dark. After stopping at the outdoor supplies store that Bud had told them about, Emily and Elizabeth traveled Highway 80 West toward Lyman. The beauty of Wyoming was breathtaking for Elizabeth. It was the first time she or Emily had been to the state. Elizabeth rolled down the windows to feel the fresh mountain wind.

"Emily, roll down your window and smell the air!" urged Elizabeth. Emily stuck her head out of the window and giggled. It seemed a lifetime ago when her parents had been killed in the car crash. She thought of them now and how they would have enjoyed the adventure that she and Elizabeth were about to embark upon. Sadness passed over her for a moment as she remembered their untimely and unexpected death. She had overcome so much grief the last couple years. *Today is another day,* she thought to herself. *Enjoy today.* "Elizabeth, I love it," she said happily. "I can't wait to see the other mustangs and to finally pick out my own horse," she said grinning.

Elizabeth watched her giggle, with the wind blowing Emily's long hair back. Elizabeth smiled at her just as the GPS announced their destination was a mile away. She hoped the trip would be a nice followup for the reporter who had done the local article on the mustangs back home. She was also worried that the training Soleil was getting would be enough to keep her solid on the trail. Bud trained his horses on cattle and out on the trail for unexpected events. Soleil was a calm horse but training was essential for her to prepare for what they might encounter in the backcountry. You needed a bombproof horse for this type of trip, one that wasn't skittish. The reporter had already met with Bud and taken her notes on what his training would be for the young horse.

Two huge posts hung in front of the entrance of the ranch with Circle T across the top of them. Elizabeth pulled the SUV in and drove down the road to the main entrance. Bud had given them perfect directions to the ranch but Elizabeth was not familiar with the area and felt it was necessary to use the car GPS. When they pulled up to the main house, they saw Soleil in the round pen. Emily was first out of the car. "Soleil, it's me, Emily," she yelled, running across the driveway to greet the mustang.

Soleil let out a nicker and ran to the fence, glad to see Emily again. *Where have you been? I thought I would never see you again.*

As Emily reunited with Soleil, Elizabeth was met by a tall man with piercing blue eyes wearing a cowboy hat.

"You must be Elizabeth," he said warmly and shook her hand. "I'm Bud McClain. Pleasure to meet you and . . ."

"Emily," the girl said shyly from the fence.

"That's some horse you've got there," he said with a grin to Elizabeth.

"Mr. McClain, did she give you a hard time?" Emily asked. "She does that sometimes to new people."

"Nothing I couldn't handle, Emily. I've been an old cowboy for a long time. Not too many tricks I haven't seen," he answered.

Elizabeth's face turned bright red. She hoped Soleil hadn't given him too hard of a time. Soleil could be a devil if she didn't know you!

"Relax, Elizabeth, and let me help you get your stuff out of the car. We'll discuss all the training over dinner. I'll show you the guest house where you and Emily will be staying."

He smiled at them and led them to the guest house.

Elizabeth had researched horse trainers and ranches in the area, and Bud McClain was recommended by locals and experts as the real horseman in this country. Word had it he once trained a horse that would kneel down for Bud to get on and then would roll over like a dog.

"See you gals at 6:30 for dinner in the main house," he said, winking at Emily. "Be on time. The Mrs. doesn't like the food to be kept waiting," he remarked as he unloaded the last of the bags and closed the door.

Elizabeth threw herself on the bed yawning. It had been a long day of traveling. "Let's get unpacked, Emily, so we can clean up for dinner."

She threw a pillow at Emily, hoisting herself up off the bed. "I have to say hello to Soleil first before dinner."

Elizabeth opened the door and looked around to see if anyone was outside before she ran out in her bare feet. She headed straight to the round pen where she had seen Soleil standing when they drove up to the main house. Elizabeth ducked between the bars and wrapped her arms around Soleil.

"Hey girl, I've missed you," she whispered as she ran her hands down Soleil's neck. "It was a long journey back, wasn't it?" she sighed, rubbing Soleil's mane.

Soleil leaned into Elizabeth and sighed, *I didn't know what was happening. I was afraid.*

"It will be worth the trip, I promise," Elizabeth stated with confidence. "I want everyone to know about the mustangs and how loyal they can be. You're gonna be just fine, girl. I know you'll be just great."

Soleil relaxed at Elizabeth's touch. She knew she would be safe now.

"Can't stay, girl, or I'll be late for dinner." Elizabeth kissed both of her eyes like she had done so many times before. She had to hurry.

Soleil stood still and watched Elizabeth run back to the guest house. *Please come back soon,* she neighed loudly to Elizabeth. *I'm ready to go and get out, and I know where the horses are.*

Chapter Three

The Mountain Cowboy

After a quick rest and freshening up a bit, Elizabeth and Emily hurried over to the main house to make sure they were not late for Mrs. McClain's dinner. Elizabeth straightened her shirt again while walking up the stairs to the main house at the Circle T. She was amazed at the size of the porch. She and Emily were staying at the guest house that was available for the guests using the ranch. The Circle T was a real working cattle ranch. The main house looked like a place that Elizabeth had only seen in magazines or read about. She had never known anyone who owned nor had she been in a home of this size. It was exhilarating as well as exciting entering the big house. The main house was a mixture of wood and stone, surrounded by a large front porch.

Emily stepped up on the porch stairs. "I've never seen a house like this," she whispered to Elizabeth. "It's so huge," she exclaimed with her mouth wide open.

The large front door opened, and Bud McClain smiled. "Welcome, ladies! You're right on time. Please come in." Elizabeth and Emily followed Bud into a large living room. "This is the great room," Bud said. "It's where everyone gathers."

Elizabeth looked around and saw beautiful leather couches with animal hides. The fireplace that ran from floor to ceiling was made from natural stone. There were large antler chandeliers hanging from the cathedral ceilings, which lighted the massive square wooden table that sat in front of the two couches.

"Please sit down. Your wrangler and guide, Michael, will be up shortly. He's out getting some stray cows that went through a broken fence in the east pasture this morning."

"A real cowboy, like the ones in movies?" Emily asked with excitement.

"I'm afraid so, Emily. Cowboy boots and all," Bud laughed.

"Dinner's ready. Everyone to the dining room," Mrs. McClain called out.

Emily and Elizabeth were led into the dining area that could seat at least 25 people. The room had one long wooden table, and it was set up with place settings for five. There was a small woman with short gray hair standing at the head of the table smiling.

"Pleasure to meet you girls. Please have a seat." Mrs. McClain motioned to Emily and Elizabeth to sit down, as she made her way back to the kitchen. "Excuse me just a moment while I finish bringing the soup in," she said quickly.

Emily sat down and looked at the table settings. There were so many forks and spoons.

As if Bud had read her mind, he said teasingly, "Don't worry, Emily. I get confused myself with all the tableware. I keep telling Mrs. McClain that I can only use one fork, spoon, and knife at time," he said, winking at Emily. Deep lines etched Bud's face with character from living a life outdoors.

Mrs. McClain returned with two more bowls of soup. "Girls, this is homemade barley soup, Wyoming style," she said smiling.

Elizabeth smiled back, picking up her soup

spoon for Emily to catch on. "Thank you, Mrs. McClain," Elizabeth said.

"Just call me Kat," the older woman said, lifting her own spoon.

Bang. The noise of a slamming door came from the living room, and Emily and Elizabeth both jumped at the sound. A tall, young man with curly brown hair came running through the doorway.

"Sorry, Mrs. McClain. I had a dickens of a time trying to find those cows out in the east pasture this afternoon!"

"Sit down, Michael, your soup will be cold by the time you tell me the story," she said warmly. "Emily, Elizabeth, this is Michael, your wrangler and guide for the next week. He's about the best there is in this part of the country." Michael took off his hat and nodded at them shyly.

"Who says so?" Bud said, grinning at Kat.

Emily looked around the table to get a good look at their wrangler.

"Something wrong, Emily?" Kat asked curiously.

"No, Mrs. McClain, just never met a real cowboy before," Emily said excitedly.

"Well Emily, you got two of the best right

here," she said laughing. "Ya'll finish your soup before the chicken gets cold. There will be a lot to talk about after dinner, and I hear that horse you have, Elizabeth, is something else. Soleil thinks she's part of the family now!"

Everyone chuckled at Kat's comment. Elizabeth looked down embarrassed. She knew she had spoiled Soleil rotten, and so did everyone else.

Michael excused himself from the table after dinner with a big grin geared toward Emily. Emily looked up and saw the tallest man she had ever seen. She couldn't help but stare at their guide. Elizabeth kicked her under the table for being rude and staring at Michael.

"Everyone to the great room," Bud announced. "I'll fill you in on the training and what I've been doing with Soleil. I've been working her on cattle, and she's a natural. Goes right after them cows. Wild horses seem to have a sixth sense about other animals."

"Kat, do you need some help clearing the table?" Elizabeth asked.

"No, thanks, Elizabeth. You go on in with Bud and Michael and discuss what Soleil has learned since she's been here, and I'll be along in a minute," she smiled warmly at Elizabeth and motioned for her to go with the rest of the bunch.

"That horse can be stubborn and was at first, until I started talking to her in her own language, release and pressure." Bud went on explaining to Elizabeth. "She thought she was going to buck me off in the beginning."

Emily was already seated on one of the large couches, asking Michael a lot of questions. Elizabeth sat down beside Emily and put her hand on Emily's leg. "Michael, I'm so sorry for all the questions but Emily is so excited to be on this trip," Elizabeth said to Michael.

"Emily was just asking me what makes a good cowboy," Michael said, grinning at Emily.

Elizabeth noticed his rough hands as he took a rope that was hanging on the wall.

"Emily, this is a lasso. Ever seen one of these?"

"You use them on cows for roping, don't you?" she asked proudly.

"A good cowboy knows how to use one real well," he said, shaking his head in agreement.

"But that's not all that makes a good cowboy, Emily," Bud said interrupting Michael. "A good cowboy . . . well . . . has a code to live by."

Emily looked puzzled. "What do you mean by a code, Bud?"

"Emily, cowboys have silent unwritten rules that they follow and live by called The Code of the West," he exclaimed. "The Code of the West is based not on myth but on the reality of life and knowing the difference between right and wrong."

Elizabeth looked over, clearly interested in these so-called codes that cowboys lived by.

"Bud, I've never heard of such codes," Elizabeth said.

Michael laughed. "You wouldn't, unless you were a cowboy," he said, flashing his sideways grin at Elizabeth with a chuckle.

Elizabeth returned the smile and turned her head toward Bud. "And just what are these codes?" she asked.

Emily was bursting to ask about these rules or codes they were talking about. "Michael, please tell us," she blurted out.

"Well, Emily, I'll name just a few and save the rest for a later time," he said while twirling the rope. "*Live Each Day With Courage, Take*

Pride In Your Work, and *Always Finish What You Start,"* he said as he looked seriously into her big brown eyes.

Blushing, Emily said, "Oh," and looked up at Elizabeth.

"Michael can give you the rest of them when you're out in the mountains, Emily," Bud said. "You'll have plenty of time to chat at camp. Camping in backcountry could be an experience for all of you. There are predators out there that will not think twice about pouncing on one of the horses. We'll need to go over some of the basics before you head out in high country, altitude being one of them. It could cause bad headaches and much more if someone was not accustomed to it."

Bud directed his attention back to Elizabeth. "Michael will be taking you to an area called Powder Rim, and after looking at the map the Bureau of Land Management gave you, Soleil was outside of the herd management area when she was captured." Leaning closer to Elizabeth and almost whispering, he added, "That horse of yours has her own rules." Bud winked at Emily as he spoke.

Elizabeth slid farther down in her seat and

thought, *Here it comes. Can't wait to hear what she's done now.*

Chapter Four

Keeping Promises

arly the next morning Elizabeth, Emily, and Bud went to the corral to saddle up Soleil. Elizabeth would need to go over what problems they may encounter on the trail but also to show her riding skills to Bud.

Working on the pressure and release would cue the horse on what she was expected to do, but Elizabeth knew Soleil needed a stern hand and rider or she would take charge. Despite her knowledge of the horse and her own riding skills, this part of the trip could be a disaster before they ever get a chance to pick out a mustang for Emily. Not to mention the follow-up article the reporter would be writing. Elizabeth froze just thinking about it. All those people who think mustangs are not trainable would have a field day with her idea of taking a wild horse that was supposed to be broken back to the wild if it didn't go well. She had to shake her mind off of the negative thoughts.

"Elizabeth, if you find Soleil jigging and wanting to run when she sees the other horses, remember to stay out of her mouth and use your legs. Keep her checked in line by using your leg behind the saddle on the side she's moving out on."

Bud climbed up on Soleil and showed Elizabeth with his leg what he was talking about. "Too many riders forget to use their legs in situations like these. Turn her around in circles and get her mind off what she's encountering." He turned the horse in circles to show her. "I worked her on cattle to teach her discipline, and she's a natural." Pushing her into a gallop, Bud sat back in the saddle, slide stopping the horse and then skidding to a halt.

"Wow, Elizabeth, look at that!" Emily said, surprised.

Elizabeth was definitely impressed with what the old cowboy had taught her horse in a few weeks.

"Now, your turn," he said, climbing down

and handing over the reins to Elizabeth.

Soleil was happy that the big man had stepped off of her and that Elizabeth was on her back again. *Hold on and watch what I can do!* Soleil took off feeling the smallest bit of pressure Elizabeth gave her, sliding to a stop and then going into a roll back with Elizabeth.

"Whoa, girl!" Elizabeth said softly. She could swear the horse was showing off. She worked the horse around the corral. When she felt the horse had softened and relaxed, she motioned for Emily to open the gate. She wanted to take Soleil out and see how she handled without any other horses around.

"Remember what I showed you," Bud said closing the gate. "Emily, let's go to the other barn and get you acquainted with Shoban. I want to see your riding skills as well. You'll like Shoban. He's the best ranch horse we have at Circle T." He laid his hands on Emily shoulders, as he watched Elizabeth and Soleil galloping out in the field. "She's a good horse, that Soleil," he said to Emily. "Solid." Bud smiled and looked at Emily. "Don't you worry at all. We'll find the right horse for you before you go home," he said in a fatherly way.

* * * * *

The next day Elizabeth, Emily, and Michael drove to Flaming Gorge National Park recreation area to park the truck and horse trailer. The reporter was there, ready to interview them and document the trip. The horses had already been saddled before loading them into the stock trailer. The truck was packed full with the camping gear they would need for the trip. The air was cool at this altitude, and the morning was clear and sunny. Michael unloaded the horses and tied them on both sides of the trailer. He had brought two of the best ranch horses Circle T owned and two pack horses for their gear. They needed good, seasoned horses with steady temperaments to accompany Soleil in the backcountry. Even well broke horses could get excited seeing a group of horses running free.

Rhonda, the reporter from *Horse News*, was already there waiting to talk to Elizabeth. Elizabeth and Emily got out of the truck to greet her.

"Hi, Rhonda. Nice to see you again," Elizabeth said cordially, shaking the reporter's hand.

"I wanted to get your thoughts before you head into the backcountry," Rhonda said, getting out her pen and pad. "How do you think Soleil will do?" she asked, looking deep into Elizabeth's eyes.

"Well . . . she IS ready for the trip. Soleil has been out here training with Bud McClain for the last few weeks. He has put her through a series of training and tests to make sure she's sound and solid before we head out, and I'm confident and trust my horse," Elizabeth said while glancing over at Soleil.

Michael was making his final tack adjustments to the horses. Emily and Elizabeth gathered up their personal saddlebags while Elizabeth talked to the reporter about the trip. "Make sure both sides are even when you're packing, and only take what you'll need for the day in your bags," Michael spoke out under his cowboy hat.

"Why just for the day?" Emily asked with a puzzled look.

"Well, Emily, we'll start climbing some steep mountains and you don't want any more weight on your horse than is necessary," Michael answered while checking his own saddlebag. "That's why we have pack horses."

Rhonda was taking notes and pictures. "Michael, any last words of wisdom before you lead this group out?" she asked with a stern look.

"Yes, happy trails," he said with a grin and continued to finish his work of getting the horses ready.

"Isn't Emily supposed to get her own mustang before you head back east?" Rhonda asked Elizabeth. "I mean, wasn't that one reason for the trip?" she added.

Elizabeth, embarrassed she had forgotten to mention that, said, "Yes, of course, we've been so excited about seeing the wild mustangs we forgot to talk about Emily's reason. Her Aunt Jenny and Uncle Phil told Emily she could pick out her own mustang at the Rock Springs facility."

Emily walked around to her horse Shoban, a black Quarter horse that had been at Circle T for 15 years. Michael lifted Emily's saddlebag over the big gelding and secured it to the saddle. By late morning the day had started to warm. Michael perspired as he adjusted Emily's stirrups.

Elizabeth made her own final adjustments also feeling the warmth of the morning. She was glad it would be cooler in the higher elevations of the mountains and was anxious to get started. Looking at the reporter and excited to get going, she said, "Rhonda, I'm sure it will be a fantastic trip all the way around!"

Elizabeth was as excited as Emily to go and see where the wild horses roamed. "Emily, if you're all packed and ready to go, why don't you lead Shoban around while I finish?" Elizabeth said, looking over at the reporter. "We're confident Soleil will be great. Please take a picture of all of us ready to go."

The reporter took a photograph of all of them before they headed out. She would meet up with them at the facility at Rock Springs where Emily would pick out a horse of her own at the end of the trip.

Michael took Shoban by the reins and hoisted Emily into the saddle. "She can just walk him out and make sure everything's to her liking. It could be a while before we will dismount for lunch. We have a full day of travel and need to get started," he said, looking directly at Elizabeth.

Elizabeth untied Soleil, looking for higher ground to mount her horse. Soleil was ready to start moving, pawing the ground. *I can smell other horses close by.*

Elizabeth took Michael's words as a hint to get moving. The three rode their horses to the trail head that would lead them up the mountain. Once they got into backcountry, cell phones would not have any reception. Michael had checked and double checked all the camping supplies for a successful trip. There would be no calls made once the group was inside the park. Michael headed for the trail head with the pack horses trailing behind. He kicked his horse and started up the mountain. There would be ranger checks in areas during their trip and places to replenish supplies.

What was left of the morning was spent climbing to higher elevations and following the old trail head. It was a slow incline, and they had not yet encountered the steep terrain. However, Michael had warned them that the difficult area was farther up. Emily could smell the unfamiliar plants when they arrived at the first open spot.

"Michael, can I pick the flowers when we stop for lunch?" she asked. The meadows were covered with tiny yellow flowers. Soleil was lathered from climbing in the altitude.

Breathing heavy from the climb, she waited before starting to graze.

Elizabeth noticed a softness that showed on the cowboy's face when Emily asked if she could pick the flowers.

"Emily, they're just beggin' for you to pick them," he said with a grin, getting off of his horse. "This looks as fine a place as any to have lunch."

Emily dismounted quickly and looked for a place to tie up the horses while they ate and so she could pick the wildflowers.

A group of pine trees stood to the left of the clearing. *It seems like a good place to tie Shoban and the rest of the horses*, Emily thought to herself. "Here, Michael, is this good?" she shouted, looking back just as a flock of birds flew out from under the brush directly at her and Shoban. Emily screamed and her horse bolted while the birds flew higher up the mountain.

"What was that?" she yelled, trying to catch hold of Shoban, who had run back to Michael. "That was grouse, or some people call 'em prairie chickens," he replied, giving Emily back her horse.

"That was scary," Emily confessed. "Didn't

know birds hung out under trees. What else hangs out under trees?" she asked hesitantly, looking for another place to tie up the horses.

"Don't ask," Elizabeth said, dismounting after all of the commotion. Soleil was good when Shoban bolted; she didn't move. Elizabeth was sure the horse had seen more than just grouse out in the wild when she was a foal. Soleil nickered with a knowing look. *Birds are the least of our worries up here.*

The three sat in silence eating their lunch, each enjoying the beauty of the rugged country sprawled out in front of them. It was God's country. Each one of them was at this place for a different reason, but coming together for a single purpose—the promise Elizabeth had made to a horse and to a little girl a long time ago.

Michael stood up after eating lunch and looked over at Emily. "Emily, remember when we spoke of cowboy codes and rules to live by?" he asked. He picked his words carefully as he spoke. "One of these rules from The Code of the West . . . well it goes . . . *When You Make A Promise, Keep It.* I think Elizabeth here is responsible for all of us being in this beautiful land and keeping her promise." He tipped his hat to Elizabeth and said, "Thank you, Elizabeth, for keeping a promise."

He moved his gaze to the horizon. "Let's get moving," he said. "We still have more riding to do before we get to base camp."

Elizabeth smiled at Michael while getting into her own saddle, feeling gratitude for the kind words he spoke. Soleil stopped grazing and looked out over the meadow thinking, *The promise was to me.*

Chapter Five

Base Camp

"Emily!" Elizabeth cried out. "Are you okay?"

Emily scampered up the steep hill, trying to grab Shoban's reins.

"I'm okay, Liz. I just wasn't ready for that climb," she said, wiping the sweat off her brow and the dust from her pants. "Michael, are we almost there?" the girl said wearily to the cowboy.

"It's just a way's up the trail, Emily. That's where we'll camp," the cowboy said, handing over Shoban's reins. "You look pale," the cowboy said to the young girl.

Emily took the horse's reins and walked up the rocky path. "I'm fine, Michael. I'm just not used to eating dirt," she said, wiping off her face. Shoban had dislodged her from the saddle while they were climbing up the steep ridge.

The mountain had jagged edges that stuck out on top of its massive peaks. The group was tired from the day's ride. Everyone was feeling the altitude except Michael. The horses looked worn out, and Elizabeth could see Soleil's rapid breathing from their climb. She looked out over the mountains and took in the scenery. The mountains were so beautiful, just breathtaking. She closed her eyes and smelled the evergreens and the forest before moving on. She did not want to forget this moment, a long-awaited moment that she had dreamed about for years.

Soleil's nostrils flared as she looked out over the same mountain range. *I need to catch my breath.*

Elizabeth headed higher up the mountain with Soleil. "Michael, when do we set up camp? The horses look tired," she said, squeezing Soleil with her legs to move forward. She led Soleil up the mountain to an open area. They had been climbing now all day, and Elizabeth was tired. The sun was going down, and all she could think about was getting off the horse.

Michael pointed to the flat area to the left of Elizabeth and Soleil. It was a spot nestled inside the mountain that would protect them from the high winds.

"Here, Michael?" Elizabeth yelled down, pointing at the flat spot. She was ready to stop, exhausted from the day's adventure. Elizabeth wanted to get the horses settled well before night set in on the mountain.

Soleil was ready to stop, too. It had been a rough climb.

Elizabeth rolled out her and Emily's sleeping bags. She had checked to make sure all of their gear was packed.

"Emily, put your things right there," she said, pointing to the back of the tent while putting linings in her and Emily's sleeping bags.

"Liz, I'm so tired," Emily yawned, throwing her belongings in the corner. "How far are we going tomorrow?" she asked.

"Michael says we'll go to the Basin, the BLM herd management area," Elizabeth answered, not taking her eyes off the sleeping bags.

"I'm hungry, Liz. Can't we do this later?" she asked.

"No, Emily, we can't. We have to help get a fire going, and that means collecting firewood so we can cook. Come on. Let's go and fetch some firewood," Elizabeth said, patting the top of Emily's head.

Michael had already started setting up the camp by tying up a line for the horses close to the tents for the night. He had hobbles for a couple of the horses. His tent was closest to the horses so he could hear if any got spooked or broke away. He worked quickly to get the horses secured before dusk.

Emily ran into the large canvas cover with an armful of kindling wood to start the fire. "Michael, I have firewood," she said excitedly.

"That's good, Emily, but leave it outside if you don't want smoke in the tents," he said, smiling at her excitement.

She put the firewood outside the large canvas that covered the tents. A coyote howled in the distance. "Liz, was that a wolf?" Emily asked wide-eyed.

"Just a coyote," Michael said, taking some firewood from her.

A shiver ran down Emily's spine from the eerie sounds. Emily ran into her tent to grab a sweater, not sure if it was the cool evening air or coyote sounds that gave her a chill.

"Let's get that fire going," she yelled.

It would be a long night if that coyote kept

howling. The last of the sun's rays disappeared behind the mountains while the three of them set up camp. Soleil had also heard the coyote. *I haven't heard that sound in a long while,* she thought. But there was more than a coyote out there. Her nose twitched from the smells.

Chapter Six

Nightfall

The moon rose over the eastern sky and cast its own glow over the mountains enveloping the shapes of the white canvas tents. Michael had prepared a cowboy cookout of steak, fried cornbread, and baked beans. Emily could smell the food cooking over the fire while she watered the horses. They had camped close to the mountain lake where water was easily accessible. The horses acted spooky close to the water, especially Soleil when Emily watered them. She ran back to camp after securing the horses back to the line that Michael had rigged up. Emily was hungry from the day's ride.

"Emily, grab yourself a plate and eat before it gets cold," Elizabeth called out.

The three ate their meals sitting around the warm campfire. There were so many unfamiliar noises for Emily and Elizabeth to get used to in the backcountry. Somewhere an owl was perched on a nearby tree and was hooting, and a lone coyote howled across the canyon every so often. Emily ate her food so quickly that she had barely tasted it. All the animal sounds had totally unnerved her.

"Liz, I'm getting ready for bed. I'm beat," she said, going into her tent. She couldn't wait to go to sleep so she couldn't hear the eerie sounds. Elizabeth and Michael finished eating and sat listening to the crackles of the fire in silence, each in their own thoughts and feeling the temperature drop several degrees once the sun had set.

"Michael, how long do you think it will be before we see the band of mustangs?" Elizabeth asked curiously.

"If we're lucky, Elizabeth, they should be over by Black Mountain this time of the year, and we'll be there tomorrow. So to answer your question, tomorrow, if we make good time," he said with a grin. "But let's get cleaned up and get to sleep. By the break of dawn I want to be saddled up. We need to get an early start."

Michael took all the dirty dishes they had

put in the basket to be cleaned in the lake. Walking down to the water, he yelled, "Get to bed, Elizabeth. I'll clean up around here."

Elizabeth walked over to her and Emily's tent. She noticed the cowboy's rifle leaning against a rock. Opening the tent, she saw Emily propped up with a candle reading.

"What are you reading?" Elizabeth asked, getting her toothbrush out of the duffel bag.

"*American Girl,*" Emily answered politely. "Do we have to listen to that coyote all night, Liz? It's giving me the creeps."

"Emily, what do you want me to do . . . go shoot it to make it stop?" Elizabeth said with a teasing tone, looking over at Emily.

"Well . . . no . . . but can you yell at it to stop or something?" Emily asked.

"Emily, it's not a dog, and a single coyote is not going to hurt you. Besides, Michael has his shotgun, and he's not going to let a coyote come and devour us," she said playfully to the frightened girl. "Now let's get to bed."

Elizabeth had finished brushing her teeth and was all washed up when she heard Michael return from the lake. "Hey, Emily's a little nervous over all of these sounds, mostly the coyote," she said smiling. "We *are* okay here, right?" she asked, looking at his expression.

"Liz, there are wild animals out here but we'll be fine. Go to bed. I'm going to check on the horses, recheck the high lines one more time, and go to bed myself. Remember this important rule in the cowboy code, *Live Each Day With Courage,*" he said grinning.

"You called me Liz" she said to the cowboy. "Only Emily ever calls me that. Good night," she said softly while going into her tent.

Elizabeth crawled into her sleeping bag and turned off the lantern.

"Emily, you sure will have one story to tell your Aunt Jenny and Uncle Phil when you get home," she said quietly to the girl. "Good night, Honey."

Soleil stirred under the moonlight. She was restless. Her nose told her there were predators close. The coyote's call was harmless to her but her instincts told her there was something more powerful lurking in the night. She neighed loudly, stamping her feet. The other horses, Shoban, Apache, and the pack horses Little Foot and Black, were starting to get restless from the mustang's pawing.

A shrill cry woke everyone from their sleep. Michael jumped up and by instinct grabbed for his gun. He heard hooves pounding out-side the tents. He ran to look where the sound had come and saw a mountain lion perched high on the rock that sheltered the tents. All of the horses had broken loose. Michael saw Shoban and Apache by the group of trees, but he did not see Soleil. The mountain lion leaped off of the rock and into the clearing where Michael stood, gun in hand.

"Michael, in front of you," Elizabeth shouted, seeing the bold mountain lion jump. Michael raised his gun to shoot when he heard a shrill noise and pounding hooves behind him. Soleil was in a full charge.

Soleil barreled down fast on the big cat, charging. Michael jumped out of the way, and the group witnessed the horse rear, striking the mountain lion. The big cat jumped over the rock into the darkness. Soleil, running head down, fled off into the nearby woods. Little Foot followed her, and the two disap-peared in the dark of the night.

"Michael, Soleil ran into the woods with the pack horse!" Elizabeth screamed. "Please help me go get her."

Emily ran past Elizabeth to catch the other two horses, tearing her pajamas on a big bush.

Pulling her pants free from the brush, Emily held tightly to her horse's halter. He was hobbled. Michael had taken hold of his own horse, Apache. The ranch horse was trained to stay close to Michael.

"She's gone!" Elizabeth yelled to Michael and Emily. "My horse is gone!"

Michael was stunned by the turn of events. He held onto his gun and followed the two horses who had disappeared into the darkness. In the distance he could hear a call from another horse, not one from their group. Elizabeth ran to Emily where she stood holding the other two horses.

"Oh, Liz," Emily said, "I have the horses. Go find Soleil and Little Foot."

Elizabeth plodded into the moonlight-filled forest. She was not afraid of the mountain lion and was determined to find her horse.

"Soleil," she yelled. Then she screamed even louder. "Please come back." Desperate now, she grabbed Michael's shirt with tight fists. "Go get her. You know where they went." Elizabeth's voice was broken.

"Elizabeth, I can hear the wild ones out there," he said, "the mustangs . . . she went to them and we cannot go after her in the dark. It's crazy to start searching now," he said wearingly.

Michael knew Soleil had fled and had gone back to the wild horses. She was wearing a halter and that was another concern. She could get caught on something and choke to death or be injured badly.

Emily and Michael watched Elizabeth sink down against the tent and cry. Emily ran to Elizabeth, "Please don't cry, Liz, please. We will find her," the girl said, choking back her own tears. "I promise we'll find her," she said to Elizabeth, taking her hand. "Let's say a prayer for her," she said, looking into Elizabeth's blue eyes. "We'll just say a prayer for Soleil to find her way home."

Elizabeth looked at the girl's big brown eyes, so innocent and filled with tears as were her own. "I know, Emily, I know. Thank you." She reached out and hugged the one person who knew what it felt like to lose something. Elizabeth had lost a horse, not her entire family like Emily had.

Chapter Seven

The Search

"What do you mean . . . Michael? We might not be able to find her in a week!" Elizabeth shouted.

"I'm just saying . . . that there's a lot of land out there, Elizabeth, and looking for one horse could take some time. The mustangs *do* go beyond the BLM herd management areas," he answered calmly.

Emily was packing up. She and Elizabeth had barely slept all night. It was early morning, and they needed to get moving. They were short two horses, and traveling would not be easy. Emily grabbed ahold of Elizabeth's hand. "Come on, Liz, we'll find her." Emily was heartbroken for Elizabeth. She of all people knew what it felt like to lose something you loved.

"I know, Emily, I just . . ." Elizabeth's voice

trailed off. Elizabeth took Soleil's saddle and swung it over the other pack horse, Black. "This is never going to fit," she said, tightening the girth and making saddle adjustments to fit the smaller pack horse. "I guess we'll just have to leave the tents and things we can't bring with us here at base camp," she said to Michael, climbing into the saddle.

Michael shook his head in agreement, looking at what they were leaving behind at camp.

The three of them took off in search of Soleil and Little Foot. The weather had turned colder, and clouds gathered across the mountains.

"It sure feels like rain," Michael said, looking up. "Never know what the weather will do at this elevation. One minute the sun is shining, and the next it's snowing."

He led them over the ridge they had camped on, hoping to find the horses in the meadow on the way to Ramsey Peak. Wild horses were always found in the high meadows this time of the year. He had just seen a group there three weeks ago on another pack trip. He didn't want Emily and Elizabeth to know how difficult it could be finding the band of horses that Soleil had joined. He also wondered if the horse would let them catch her again this time. He shook his head and told himself, *Michael, just stay in the present.*

Riding at this altitude, Emily could see for miles across the mountains. The view was spectacular but the wind was blowing very hard. Emily looked back at Elizabeth.

"Liz, you okay?" she asked. "You look so . . . sad," the girl said in her sweet voice, trying to hold her hat down and talk at the same time. Elizabeth looked tired and weary. Emily knew what Soleil meant to her. Soleil was everything to Elizabeth.

"I'm okay, Emily," Elizabeth said, managing a smile. "Thank you for asking."

"Michael, do you know where or close to where the horses could take Soleil?" she asked, trying not to sound nervous.

"I'm guessing they will go to the other side of that ridge," he said pointing. "Over yonder where the big rock hangs over the canyon. It's called Black Mountain."

"What do you mean, you guess?" Elizabeth asked with her voice rising in alarm. "You said you knew where the horses and the BLM's herd management areas were located." She had tried so hard to keep in control but was losing it. She took her horse and rode past Emily so she could see Michael's face.

"Elizabeth, there are a dozen places the horses could go . . . that I know of, but like I said earlier, finding which one in five days may not be possible. But we will do our best, Elizabeth. Try and stay focused and calm," he said to her in a comforting way.

"I'm sorry, Michael," Elizabeth confessed. "I don't mean to sound so childish but I waited so long to have another horse. Soleil was a gift . . . when she finally came along. The thought of losing her . . . what if she got injured, I would never forgive myself."

Elizabeth looked long and hard at the cowboy. She could hear her words echo off the mountain. Michael looked mysterious under his black hat and bandanna. He never looked up while he was riding. He just focused on the task at hand. The two rode their horses side by side for a while—neither saying a word; the only sounds were from the horses clopping against the rocky path. Elizabeth glanced back at Emily and tried to smile to comfort herself more than Emily.

The rocky path stopped and was replaced

with tall grass. Raindrops hit their hats with a pitter-patter sound. The rain started slow at first but soon became full force. Michael led the group down the valley into a canopy of evergreen trees to get out of the rain.

"Emily, Elizabeth, tuck in here with your horses," he said, riding in behind them. "Just underneath the tall trees we may find a spot to get out of the worst of this rain," he added, pushing his way inside the canopy.

"I hope this doesn't get any worse," Emily said, looking up at the sky. The clouds were dark and low, and fog was settling around the mountain. "This doesn't look good, does it, Michael?" Emily asked. The girl hardly got the words out before hail started falling. Golf ball-sized hail was landing all around them.

"Follow me," Michael yelled to Elizabeth and Emily. "There's a small cave just up the crest of that mountain over there, but we have to cross Bitter Creek that runs down to the valley."

He took his horse and cantered along the tree line toward the base of the mountain. Emily and Elizabeth followed the cowboy, trying to keep up with his horse. Elizabeth couldn't see anything from underneath her hat except the front of her horse. The hail had stopped but the wind was so powerful that a few tree limbs had broken off and lay in the path in front of them.

"Michael, slow down," she yelled, her voice drowning in the wind. "We can't see you in this weather," she added, looking back to see how close Emily was behind her. Elizabeth was uncomfortable riding the pack horse. The horse didn't feel right, and all she could think about was Soleil. When her thoughts were just about to consume her, she looked up and saw a horse and rider galloping toward her. Michael was there in an instant, and she noticed he looked uncomfortable riding up.

"Elizabeth, hurry up and stay behind me," he managed to yell in the wind. "This storm is dangerous, and we need to get to the cave on Hunter's Bluff where there is shelter."

Emily and Elizabeth looked at the cowboy, neither knowing what to do next but follow his lead. The three weaved in and out with their horses around fallen tree limbs and slowly made their way to the creek. Michael led the group down the bank and into the raging water.

"Be careful. The crossing is not deep here

but stay in the middle," he directed. "It drops off on either side."

Michael plunged into the swiftly moving water with his horse, looking back at Elizabeth and Emily to make sure they were following as he had ordered them. He was the one responsible for the group and for keeping them safe. He already felt bad enough that Elizabeth's horse had taken off and vowed to himself that this would be the last of the bad luck for them. He thanked God that the hail had stopped and it was only raining now.

"Elizabeth, please help me," Emily cried out. "Liz!" she screamed.

Emily's horse, Shoban, had tripped on the rocky bed and fell into the deep water. Emily was thrown off the horse into the swift current. Michael and Elizabeth turned around just as the girl went under the water.

"Michael!" Elizabeth screamed in the loudest voice she could find.

The cowboy jumped off his horse and dove into the water after Emily. He reached her quickly and pulled her to safety.

"Emily?" he asked the girl. She looked so small in his arms. "Are you hurt?"

"Yes . . . no, I'm just scared," she answered,

clinging to him.

"Oh Emily . . . come here," Elizabeth motioned to her. "I can't lose you, too!" She held Emily close to her.

"How far is it, Michael? Emily's soaked." She grabbed Emily and took a blanket off of her horse to wrap her in. "Emily, you're shaking."

"The cave isn't too far so let's get going if everyone's okay," Michael said, looking at Elizabeth. "Emily's horse looks fine, but she can ride with me. She'll stay warmer that way."

"Elizabeth . . . what if Soleil gets caught by the BLM again?" Emily asked.

"Emily, remember the tattoo Soleil carries on her neck?" Elizabeth asked. "That tattoo is an alpha numeric code that the U.S. Government gave Soleil when she was captured, and that's her registration number. It's her identification number. If she gets caught again, they'll know who adopted her and where she was adopted, too." This seemed to quiet Emily for the moment.

Elizabeth noticed the trail head that lead up the mountain was worn and well used. She followed behind Michael, leading Emily's horse. Around the bend, tucked away on the side of the hill, was a small cave. The opening looked like it had been bored into the mountain with a modern-day tool, and it was large enough for all of them to get inside safely.

"Wait here, Emily. I want to be sure none of the local animals have taken up residence inside the cave." Michael dropped Emily down and rode up, gun in hand, into the cave opening. He peered out the cave mouth and motioned that the cave was clear.

Elizabeth and Emily led their horses into the opening. Elizabeth sat against the cave wall in exhaustion with her head deep in her hands. Michael shook her arm.

"Hey, we have to make a fire and get Emily dry. Will you help me?"

He took her arm, helping her rise. He couldn't help but notice how tired she looked.

"Come on. Let's find firewood," he said gently to her. He looked over at Emily and said, "Important cowboy rule . . . *Do What Has To Be Done.*" He held Emily's gaze for a moment and said, "Never forget that rule."

Chapter Eight

Free

Soleil plunged through the darkness in the familiar terrain where she had once run free. She tried to distance herself from the mountain lion that had attacked them in camp. The horse's instincts were still sharp. Being in captivity for the past few years had not taken away her survival skills. The wind had picked up, and she could smell a storm coming. The land was harsh in the mountains, and a summer storm could be deadly to a horse. Horses often got struck by lightning trying to find shelter under a tree.

Soleil used her instincts to guide her. Her nose told her that there was a herd of horses not far ahead. *I know where I am. I've been here before.* She led Little Foot through a rocky path that led down from the camping area. The trail that led from the mountain faded into a grassy meadow, and soon Soleil heard the sound of a horse nearby. *I know that smell!* She neighed in response to the sound and was met with another horse's neigh. She picked up her pace, anxious to find the safety of another herd. She stopped and lifted her head to listen. She could hear the sounds of horses approaching her. Little Foot nickered nervously to Soleil's reaction. Soon the two were surrounded by a small group of horses.

The stallion, a palomino, sniffed the new horses. He snorted at Soleil, the big mare with a golden mane, and at the smaller paint horse. The three horses stood facing each other until the stallion charged forward, screaming a loud neigh for them to follow him. The small group ran a short distance in the night to a herd that was waiting in the tall grassy meadow. Soleil felt herself shaking from fear but followed the stallion.

The mountain lion roared in the distance. Soleil turned her head to the sound, remembering what had happened earlier at camp. Instincts taking over, Soleil went to the grazing herd. Just like years earlier, the herd moved closely with the land in the mountains. Something didn't feel right. It was her land, her herd, but something was missing. *I'm not wild anymore,* she thought. *I live with man now.*

The storm came quick and hard. Hail fell from the thunderous clouds. The herd moved to the safety of the tall evergreens to protect them from the ice balls. They would wait out the storm there.

Soleil looked over the herd. Seeing some of her old herd on the mountain, she recognized the old mare and made her way through the group to where the old horse stood. They touched noses briefly. The old mare instantly remembered her foal. She whinnied softly to Soleil and nuzzled her neck; they were both happy to see each other after many years apart. *I thought I would never see you again,* she neighed to her mother. The two stood nose to nose waiting for the storm to end. Soleil was tired from all of the confusion, and this time she had found safety with the herd. She felt like a small foal again by her mother's side. She dropped her head and slept. She was once again home with her mother and the herd. Her father, the big bay stallion that had protected them, was missing. The palomino stallion was in charge now.

The morning rose with the break of dawn,

and the horses were on the move to the higher meadow. Soleil followed close to the old mare that led them up the mountain to the summer grasses. *Where is she taking us?* she wondered. The sun rose higher while the horses stopped in the meadow to graze. The rains had left their mark on the summer grasses, leaving droplets of water shining in the early light. The horses would stay close to the meadow where the grazing would be good for a few weeks and the spring foals could grow strong. Soleil and Little Foot settled in with the herd, filling their bellies with the summer grass. She was at last free and with the herd, but something was missing: *Elizabeth, the woman who had loved her and taught her to trust man, was missing.*

Chapter Nine

Riding the Ridge

Michael had made a small campfire close to the cave's opening, so the smoke would not fill the cave. Elizabeth walked over to Emily, bringing her some hot tea.

"Emily, sweetheart, drink this tea. It will help warm you." The girl was almost dry. "You okay?" she asked tenderly, stroking Emily's hair and combing it with her fingers. Her hair was a rich chestnut brown and hung down her back. Elizabeth loved looking into the big brown eyes that stole her heart several years back. "Oh Emily, I feel terrible! I thought this trip would be exciting but I think I bit off more than I could chew this time."

"Liz, stop worrying! Let's just find Soleil. I'll be fine, I swear. I'm not a baby anymore, and I can handle being thrown from a horse and a little water," she said, sipping her tea.

Elizabeth looked at her like a mother would, to see if she was telling the truth. "I guess that's true, God help us."

"Elizabeth, I'm going back to get the rest of the camping equipment for the night," Michael said. Pointing at the mountain in front of them, he added, "We're going to have to go over that big ridge, to get to the other meadow where Soleil may have gone, and I don't think we should be crossing that river again tonight."

Michael looked over at the two huddled against the wall. He took his bags off the horses and laid them in the back of the cave. "We have to get to the ranger station tomorrow to pick up some more supplies. I'm going to head out now, so I can get back before suppertime. Unpack the bags and let the things dry out from Emily's belongings."

Then he pulled out a Winchester shotgun and handed it to Elizabeth. "Don't use this unless you have to, but have it ready."

"Michael, be careful!" Emily yelled, pulling off her wet socks.

"You bet I will, and I'll be back before long," he said, winking at her. Tipping his hat to Elizabeth and Emily, he left the cave.

Michael also wanted to get a good look around for signs of the horses. They did not have time to lose, and he could move more quickly alone.

Michael doubled back and led his horse to the top of the ridge. The weather had broken, and he could see the area called the Red Desert Basin across the mountain. He pulled his binoculars out and scanned the land looking for horses. No sign of the two horses or any other horses within range of the Basin. His only chance was to go back to base camp and see if he could pick up something he missed earlier in the crazy scene to find Soleil. He headed down from the steep mountain around the cave where Elizabeth and Emily waited and headed for the spot in the river the three had crossed earlier. Once he reached more level land, traveling would be easier. He broke his horse out in a lope, jumping over the small trees and limbs. He reached the river bed shortly and walked his horse over without an incident. Out of the river he headed out again at a fast trot to make use of the daylight he needed to track Soleil.

He picked up on some horse tracks not far

from their base camp. Michael followed the tracks until they disappeared on the rocky mountain terrain. He rode up farther and found a group of horse tracks moving east. If the herd was moving east, it could be where he thought the herd would be this time of year over at Red Desert Basin. Once he made it to the ridge of the mountain, he followed it along the top to where he could see the lower area that spread out to the valley. He pulled out his binoculars and scanned the valley below, and there under the hot summer sun were the horses . . . grazing.

Michael could see them. He couldn't make out if Soleil was among them but he would have bet his best horse that she was with this herd. The valley basin was too far for him to travel today. He would lose the daylight making such a journey this time of day. Michael turned back toward the old campsite to collect the rest of their camping gear. He needed to hustle and let Elizabeth know where Soleil had gone. It would not be an easy trek going over to the Basin. The path over the ridge was steep and rocky. It would take them at least one full day of traveling just to reach it, and there were a number of hiding places where the horses could be in the BLM's herd management areas.

Back at the cave Elizabeth had dried out Emily's clothing and had unpacked the saddlebags. She had gotten Emily changed into some dry clothes and took on the job of fixing them something to eat.

"Emily, are you hungry? I'm starving," she said, looking for a can of soup or something to fix for them. "Where are those pans he used for dinner?" she mused out loud. Rummaging through the equipment she had packed, she found a pan and a can of soup. "Ahhhh, here we go," she said as she opened the can and poured its contents into the pan.

"Wow, this day seems to go on forever," Emily said, wiping her hands on her pants.

"What . . . finding Soleil or being out here by ourselves?" Elizabeth asked.

"About finding Soleil . . . what if we don't?" Emily asked.

"Can't and don't do not belong in my dictionary, Emily. Going home without Soleil is not an option, and we WILL find her," Elizabeth said strongly.

"I hope so, Liz," Emily said as she broke out in tears. "I'll never forgive myself if we don't," she said through her sobs.

"Oh, Emily, how could it be your fault? You had no control over a mountain lion," Elizabeth tried to comfort her.

"I knew the horses were spooked at something when we watered," Emily answered still crying.

Elizabeth brought her a cup of hot soup. "Hush now, thinking like that is just plain crazy. If anyone is at fault, it should be me. I should have known better than to bring a wild horse back to the country she came from to begin with . . . like she would choose ME over a herd of wild horses. I must be living in fantasy land!" Elizabeth sat down next to Emily and put her arm around her. "It's neither of our faults, Emily," Elizabeth said, looking her in the eyes. "Do you hear me? It's neither of our faults!"

Emily buried her head next to Elizabeth and cried softly. She was tired and just wanted to find Soleil. *This trip was supposed to be fun,* she thought. "But Soleil isn't wild anymore," she said softly to herself.

Elizabeth kept herself busy, getting the cave together for the night. She gathered more firewood and laid out her and Emily's sleeping bags. Emily had fallen asleep curled up by the fire. All Elizabeth could think about was finding Soleil. She hoped the horse had not been wounded in the encounter with the mountain lion. Elizabeth looked outside and saw the day slipping away. She looked at her watch. It was almost seven o'clock and would get dark in the canyon soon. *Where's Michael?* Elizabeth thought. *Did he find Soleil?* She had to get outside because she was driving herself crazy.

She walked outside and looked over the bluff that held the cave. Even in the rain, it was so beautiful in the mountains. The mountains were not this rustic back east. The sun was just settling its pink and amber glow on the bare rock mountaintops. She held her hands close to her heart, looked up, and then closed her eyes, with her words broken and pleading. "Please God, don't let me lose Soleil, and please keep us all safe," she prayed quietly.

The horses neighed softly, and Elizabeth opened her eyes and saw Michael coming around the bend with their camping supplies. The horses heard him before she saw him.

"Michael, thank God you got back. I was

getting worried," she said as she ran down the path to meet him. "Well, did you find her?" she asked anxiously.

"No, I didn't find her but I know where she went," he answered softly, climbing the embankment to the cave.

"Where is she? Did you see her?" Elizabeth said anxiously, following close behind.

"I'll tell you all about it. Let's get the stuff in and some dinner going. I'm starving," he said as he jumped off his horse and unpacked the supplies. "Where's Emily?" he asked.

"Asleep. Poor kid is worn out."

"How about you?" he asked her.

"No, but I'm about to lose my mind if you don't tell me where Soleil went," she answered coolly.

"Okay, okay, I'll tell you over dinner. Come help me get the camp things in and dinner going and then I WILL TELL YOU EVERY-THING, I promise," he answered, carrying supplies to the cave. He was relieved he had found the horses and could tell Elizabeth something.

Chapter Ten

Open Range

Early the next morning Michael, Elizabeth, and Emily headed out for their long ride to Red Desert Basin. Michael was glad the rain had come yesterday and wet the land. It had been dry this summer, and the storms could start fires this time of year. "Michael, will you tell me more *cowboy codes?*" Emily asked.

"How about *Talk Less And Say More,*" he said, turning around on his horse and smiling at Emily's response.

"That's not one . . . is it?" Emily said back to him.

"It certainly is, Emily, and a good one to remember," he said, turning his horse again and riding on.

"Liz, what did he mean by that?" Emily asked in a low voice. "That I talk too much?"

"It means pick and choose your words carefully, Emily, and get to the point. Don't just ramble with empty words. Mean what you say, and say what you mean." Elizabeth answered her and then looked ahead for Michael, who had stopped with his binoculars to scan the lower valley for the horses.

"Do you see them?" Elizabeth asked.

"No, I don't but that doesn't mean they're not out there. As I said earlier, there are many places that can hide them," he answered her, not taking his eyes from the binoculars. "We'll make camp on the other side of this mountain tonight, so let's get moving. We can eat lunch in the saddle and water the horses when we make it down to the campsite. There's a small lake at the bottom where we'll water and make camp. We'll be close to the area where I saw them yesterday."

The group made the grueling ride down the ridge to the valley where the lake was nestled. The open country was surrounded by the mountains and was just breathtaking for Elizabeth. She took in the picture of the serene setting—the clear lake, the golden grasses, and the tall evergreens that engulfed the meadow. She now understood why Soleil would want to stay here. It was beautiful.

Dismounting from her horse, she led him to the lake and took out her canteen to drink. So many things were going through her mind she couldn't turn them off. *Would Soleil come to her or run away? What if she was injured and had to be put down?* As if Michael had read her mind, he said, "Stop worrying, Elizabeth, we'll find her. Worst case scenario she gets captured again by the BLM. They'll know who she belongs to when they check her brand."

"Michael, don't you understand? What if she doesn't choose me! What if she would rather be free and in this country than in a two-acre pasture back east where she can't run free?" Elizabeth almost choked on her words getting them out. "I wouldn't want to go back if I could live here and be free," she blurted out with angry words.

"Elizabeth, what are you angry about? Are you angry at me?" he said, putting his hand on her shoulder and turning her to face him.

"No, Michael. I'm angry with me," she said, looking down in a beaten voice.

"Elizabeth, this rule is for you. *Know Where To Draw The Line*," he said to her in a calm and reassuring voice. "That one is about drawing the line between right and wrong, and you, my friend, are thinking wrong. Now get your horse's tack off and let's set up camp. Tomorrow will be a big day, and I need your mind right."

He looked over at Emily playing in the water, acting like she hadn't a care in the world. He smiled at Elizabeth and said, "See through the eyes of a child."

"Elizabeth, what are we going to tell the reporter?" Emily asked

Elizabeth didn't say a word. She didn't know. What would she tell Emily's Aunt Jenny and Uncle Phil about the so-called tamed Soleil who took off again and was running with the wild ones? They might not be so agreeable for Emily to get a mustang if this didn't turn out well.

After the three had set up camp and tied another highline for the horses, Emily and Elizabeth went to take a swim in the lake and clean up. The water looked so refreshing.

"Wow, wouldn't this be great, Liz, if we could do this every day?" Emily asked while she floated on the lake.

"I was thinking more of a hot shower myself," Elizabeth said, pondering Emily's words. "This water is so cold my teeth are starting to rattle! Let's get dressed and ready for dinner. I'm beat, Emily."

Michael had their supper ready when the girls walked into camp. Elizabeth could smell the beans and cornbread cooking from the lake. Each took a plate and sat without saying a word to each other until they were all finished. Elizabeth grabbed the dishes and noticed that Michael had hobbled his horse instead of tying him and the horse had bells around its neck.

"Why do you have the bells?" she asked him with a questioningly look.

"Because if I hear him, all is good and I know he hasn't wandered off. Sometimes horses can learn how to move with the hobbles on anyway," he answered.

Emily and Elizabeth pulled their sleeping bags out of the tent and decided to sleep under the stars by the campfire. It was a beautiful night by the mountain lake. The stars were so bright that you could see the constellations. It was quiet by the fire, and all that could be heard were a splash in the water from time to time from a trout that had feasted on some unfortunate creature and a hoot owl in the distance. Bells could be heard from one horse grazing, and the fire crackled down as the three of them slept under the open range.

Elizabeth thought she was dreaming of horses neighing and jumped at the sound of the neigh, but she wasn't dreaming. It was dawn, and Michael had already saddled the horses.

"What time is it?" Elizabeth asked, looking at her watch.

"Time to get going and start looking for that horse of yours," he said clearly in a hurry.

"Emily, wake up, Sweetheart," Elizabeth said, gently shaking her.

"Ooohhh . . . I'm sleepy," Emily said, rubbing her eyes. "And sore," she added, clearly making a painful face after sitting up.

"There's hot coffee on the fire, Elizabeth, and we need to get moving to reach Red Desert Basin this afternoon," said Michael.

Chapter Eleven

Leaving the Herd

"Elizabeth, look!" Michael handed the binoculars to Elizabeth.

Elizabeth looked through the lenses, scanning the area where Michael was pointing. "There they are!" she said, not taking her gaze off the horses.

Michael was already headed toward them at a slow trot. "Let's get closer," he said, looking back for Elizabeth and Emily to follow.

On the far side of the mountain where they were riding, a group of twelve to fifteen mustangs were grazing on the mountain. The trees made it hard to see all of the horses but several were right in front of them.

"Will they start running if they see us?" Emily asked.

"They already know we're here, Emily," Michael said, looking again in the binoculars to see if he could spot Soleil. "We just can't spook them. We have to get close but not too close," he said, trying to see if he could spot Soleil. "Let's set up camp over there," he said, pointing to the bluff about a quarter mile ahead.

The three made their way to the camping spot, and Elizabeth was nervous the horses would take off.

"How are we going to get closer?" she asked.

"We're not," he answered. "First, we need to make sure Soleil is with them. So far I haven't spotted her but that doesn't mean she isn't there." he said, getting off his horse. "Let's set up camp and then see if we can't double around to see if Soleil is with this herd. It could be late when we get back, and it looks like it's going to rain. I want to use it to our advantage to get closer to the horses."

Emily was so excited to see the wild horses. "Liz, can I take pictures if we can get close enough?"

Elizabeth was so anxious to find Soleil and see if she was with this herd that she didn't even hear Emily. She never answered.

"Liz, can I take photos?" Emily said again, loudly.

"I'm sorry, Emily. I was just thinking of the best way to get Soleil to come to me. Yes, yes, of course, this is your trip just as much as mine, Emily, and I'm sorry it seems that it's been all about Soleil . . . really I am. I'm excited to help you pick out your own mustang."

"Thank you, Liz. Let's just find Soleil first," Emily said as she smiled at Elizabeth.

Elizabeth smiled back and said, "You are one great kid!"

The three had climbed to a high spot where they could see over in the meadow where the horses were grazing. Michael scanned the area with the binoculars and then handed them to Elizabeth, shaking his head. She took them and was still for a long time just looking.

"Do you see something I don't?" he asked her.

"Probably not. I don't see Soleil if that's what you're asking!" she said, handing the binoculars back to him and looking defeated.

"Can I see them?" Emily asked. "Wow, did you see that big P

alomino?" she said excitedly. "I sure would love to have him," she said in a dreamy way, never taking her gaze off the horses.

Elizabeth didn't say a word. She just got up and started walking back to camp. Soleil wasn't with these horses, and she just couldn't think of going home without her, much less look for another mustang and talk about it with Emily right now. Emily was excited as she should be. It wasn't Emily's fault Soleil was gone.

"Liz, where you going?" Emily said looking up.

"I'm going back to camp now to figure this out. Why don't you stay with Michael and finish getting the photos that you wanted? You should be able to get some good shots from here."

Elizabeth needed some time to herself. She really thought she would find Soleil with the other horses.

"We'll stay a little bit and look some more. Maybe she is close by. Tomorrow we have to check in at the ranger station and pick up some more supplies," Michael said, getting up himself. "Do you have your whistle?"

"Yes, I have it. I'll be fine. It's not that far, and I'll blow it if I see anything," she said, clearly upset.

Elizabeth walked back to camp feeling overwhelmed. She sat down crying and thinking, *We never really own anything, do we? We just borrow it.* Her thoughts were going crazy. *Oh, Soleil, please come back.* She was sobbing now. She hadn't cried this hard in years. She got up and started calling Soleil's name. "Soleil, you always came when I called you," she said, calling her name louder. "Soleil."

Emily and Michael returned to camp to see Elizabeth just sitting on a rock drawing circles in the sand.

"Liz, I got some good shots of the horses," she said excitedly.

Elizabeth managed a smile. "I can't wait to see them, honey." Then, looking at Michael, she added, "So what's the plan now, cowboy?"

Michael knew this was coming. Taking off his hat, he said, "Like I said, let's get to the ranger station in Sweetwater and we'll let the Forest Park know that Soleil is missing. They can alert the Bureau of Land Management's Rock Springs facility and let them know the area where we were camping."

Elizabeth shook her head in agreement. It was getting dark, and they needed to rest the horses and eat something. "You have any more cowboy rules that could fit this situation?" she said half-jokingly.

"As a matter a fact, I do . . . *Remember That Some Things Aren't For Sale,*" he said, putting his gear away. "To a cowboy, the best things in life aren't things. Now let's get ready for supper."

Everyone had eaten and washed up. Elizabeth had opted to sleep outside so she could see the stars and feel the fire. She lay there for hours just looking at the star constellations, thinking about Soleil and if she was okay, before she fell asleep.

* * * * *

Soleil had heard Elizabeth call her from a far distance. Her ears were erect, and she was restless. She moved through the horses that stayed on the far side of the mountain. *I need to find my way back.* She took off at a trot.

The old mare lifted her head to see where the younger horse, her foal, was going. Soleil went to the edge of the forest. She turned her head to look at the old mare one more time. The two stood looking at each other for a moment, each remembering the bond they

shared. Soleil nickered, *"I will never forget you."*
She turned and found the trail head at the
edge of the forest that would lead her back
to the mountain where she had fled. The old
mare stood and looked at the path Soleil had
taken as if she had anticipated her to return
before she put her head down and continued
to graze.

Elizabeth thought she was dreaming again
when she heard the sound of a horse's nicker.
She was so tired she couldn't wake up until
she heard footsteps running by her. Dazed
and groggy, she thought the mountain lion
had returned when she saw Michael.

Michael was moving toward the horses
when Soleil came crashing into camp at a
dead run.

"Soleil!" Elizabeth said in disbelief. "Oh
sweet Jesus, what made you come back?" She
jumped up from her sleeping bag, grabbing
the horse, rubbing her hands over her, and
feeling for injuries. Satisfied the horse was
fine, Elizabeth buried her head in Soleil's
mane and wept. *I was with my herd, my mom,*
the horse nickered, standing quietly while
Elizabeth made a fuss over her.

"I can't believe it!" Michael said, moving

quickly to the horse to grab her halter. Looking in Soleil's eyes, "I thought for sure, girl, you would be tough to catch."

Michael looked over at Elizabeth with pride in his eyes. "You did something right, Elizabeth . . . she found us," he said to both of them while leading Soleil back to the other horses. He was grinning from ear to ear at them. "Happy to be back, girl?"

It was sad leaving, Soleil thought, *but I'm sure happy I found Elizabeth.* Elizabeth belonged to her as far as Soleil was concerned.

Chapter Twelve

Finding Aspen

The three of them made it back to the McClains' Circle T Ranch without any more incidents. It took them two days to get back, and they were lucky that they only lost the pack horse, Little Foot, and no one had been injured. Michael would probably get Little Foot back in the next couple of weeks. He will bring one of the range hands to help capture him before the BLM roundup next year.

Other than being physically tired from the trip, everyone was relieved and happy to be in a real bed and have a hot shower. Michael was more than happy that they didn't have to make the trip to Powder Rim. It was outside the BLM's herd management area and hard to navigate over the rugged mountains. Making it back to the ranger station for supplies and to phone the ranch to let the McClains know that all was well was a journey in itself. What a story Elizabeth and Emily would have to tell when they went home. The laughter and raised brows that came from Bud when they retold the story of Soleil, the mountain lion, Emily falling into the river, and Soleil finding them at camp were surreal. Now the task at hand was going to Rock Springs to pick out a mustang for Emily, one of the main reasons for the trip.

* * * * *

Emily ran out of their guest house to the car they had rented at the airport earlier that week. She opened the door and was excited to finally be going to one of the BLM's holding facilities for the mustangs. She was finally able to pick out her own horse, and it would stay at the McClains' ranch for a month with Soleil being gentled and trained.

"Hurry up, Elizabeth," Emily hollered to Elizabeth. "Let's go." She was so excited she couldn't sit still. "That reporter lady will be waiting to get the story about our trip," she managed to say without sounding too anxious.

"Emily, how happy are you?" Elizabeth said to her as she was climbing into the big SUV.

"Happy . . . I'm finally getting a mustang!" she beamed with excitement.

"Yes, you are. Let's wait for Michael and Bud to lead us to Rock Springs with the horse trailer. They know where they're going, and we don't," she said to Emily smiling.

She put her hand on the young girl's arm and gave a quick squeeze. The two had grown closer on their trip, learning more about themselves and each other than they thought possible. "You know, Emily, when I got Soleil I was just as happy as you are now."

Elizabeth followed closely behind Michael and Bud to the facility at Rock Springs. Emily was the first one out of the car, practically sprinting to the large gate.

"Emily, wait for us. Remember what I told you," Elizabeth warned.

The reporter was waiting by the entrance of the facility.

"*Be Tough But Be Fair,*" Michael blurted out to Elizabeth when she got out of the truck. "Another rule in The Code of the West."

"And what does that mean?" Elizabeth said to him with a questionable look.

"Fair play is deeply engrained in a cowboy's life," Michael continued to talk. "Tell the reporter the whole story, Elizabeth. Be fair and give her the full version for her article. Don't be afraid to tell the truth is all I'm saying," he said quietly, walking with Elizabeth.

"Elizabeth," the reporter called out from the front gate, "it seems everybody made it just fine?" she asked, looking a little intense. "Was the trip what you had expected?"

"Yes, we're all fine," Elizabeth answered her calmly.

"How did your horse do? Was Soleil as solid as you thought?" she asked, writing as she spoke.

"Soleil did just great. The trip was a little more exciting than I thought it would be but Soleil pulled through when I needed her," Elizabeth answered, winking at Emily and Michael.

"Could you be more specific?" the reporter asked her.

"Yes, of course, we'll get to that but first I have one little girl who has waited patiently to pick out her horse. So let's get this documented first, and we'll go over some of the trip details later," Elizabeth answered, holding onto Emily's hand.

The five of them looked at the horses in the corrals, walking and making a mental note on the horses they liked from the Wyoming group of mustangs. In the last corral on the far end there was a small dapple colt about a year old with the longest black mane Emily had ever seen. His mane was matted, and he was skinny but he had a kind eye, as Elizabeth would say, and was not afraid when they walked up to the fence. He didn't look very big but his hooves were huge for his size.

"Emily, there's your horse," Bud said, pointing at the colt. "He has nice confirmation and a good foundation," Bud said, looking the colt over. "No foot, no horse, is what we say out here," he added finally.

"Bud knows his horse flesh," Michael said, grinning at Emily. "One important cowboy rule is *Ride For The Brand*, and that brand, Emily, on the side of his neck pretty much says it all. A real mustang captured by the United States Government."

Emily looked into the eyes of the gray colt. His mane was black against his gray color, and his tail was long and wavy. His tail mimicked his mane with streaks of white through it. He was beautiful, and she knew he was for her.

"Oh Elizabeth, I want him," she said with pleading eyes. "And I'm going to name him Aspen because of his coloring. Gray white like the bark on the Aspen trees."

"Well Emily, I think that's a great idea. Let's take him . . . shall we?" she said, hugging Emily tightly as she thought, *Here we go again . . . another one!*

The End

Acknowledgements

Photographer
Lisa Crosby

www.lisacrosby.com (website);

Lisacrosby79@yahoo.com (email)

Lisa Crosby's photograph of Soleil was featured on the cover of my first book, Soleil, A Mustang's Story. As shown above, her original photograph of Three Amigos inspired me the first time I saw it. I knew the minute I laid eyes on this picture that I wanted it on the book cover for *Soleil's Journey Home*. Lisa's photographs always move me with a story only a wonderful photographer can tell with visuals alone. I'm honored to have Lisa's work on my book covers as well as in my heart.

Illustrator
Shelia Walker
sheliawalker.com (website);
sheliafayewalker@gmail.com (email)

Sheila has been a dear friend of mine for many years and I've always been an admirer of her art. When I first decided to write *Soleil, A Mustang's Story*, I knew her realistic illustration style would perfectly capture the essence of the story. In a series of pencil and oil dry brush drawings, she brings each character to life with great skill, imagination and attention to detail – a true testament to Shelia's ability as an artist. I'm proud of our work together and look forward to working together on future projects.

Editors
Kathy and Vivian

Kathy worked with me on *Soleil's, A Mustang Story*, and I wanted her on board for Soleil's

Journey Home. Kathy's suggestions really made me think about the storyline and challenged me with questions that had my mind spinning with the correct answers. During the editing of this book Kathy also lost her mother and was not able to finish as planned. I am very thankful for her help and insight with the process. Another dear friend suggested Vivian, and I appreciate her stepping in to assist me with proofreading on short notice.

Family and Friends

I thank all of my family and friends for their encouragement and giving me the chance to live my dream. I could not have accomplished this book without their love and support. I also would like to give special thanks to the United States Wild Horse & Burro Association and the Bureau of Land Management's wild horse program for information, support, and maps needed for this book. Last, but certainly not least, I could have never accomplished this without my friend and husband, Ken, and all of his support and guidance.

Inspiration

My inspiration always starts with the horses. In addition, one of my biggest inspirations is from John Wayne's famous words: "A man's got to have a code, a creed to live by, no matter what his job," which have always stayed with me. Cowboy codes were first chronicled by the famous Western writer Zane Grey in his 1934 novel, *The Code of the West*, and Ramon Adams, the Western historian who wrote *The Cowman and His Code of Ethics* in 1969. It wasn't till I came across the book *Cowboy Ethics* by James R. Owen that I thought about applying these unwritten cowboy rules to *Soleil's Journey Home*. The cowboy codes in *Cowboy Ethics* fit in perfectly with the story, lessons in life, and something more Elizabeth and Emily could learn on the trail. In *Soleil's Journey Home*, the unwritten codes were taken from the ten codes of conduct in *Cowboy Ethics: What Wall Street Can Learn from the Code of the West* (page 24) by James R. Owen. Thank you, Jim Owen, for allowing me to use your ten codes in this book.

Conclusion

Soleil's Journey Home is the second in a series of books about a wild mustang. For readers interested in learning more about the wild mustangs, or how to help them, sponsor, or adopt them, check the following resources.

Resources

Bureau of Land Management
Wild Horse and Burro Program
1-866-4Mustangs
www.wildhorseanburro.blm.gov

United States Wild Horse & Burro Association
Robin Rivello President
23 Hooker Street
Jamesburg NJ 08831
president@uswhba.org

Black Hills Sanctuary
P.O. Box 998
Hot Springs, SD 57747
1-800-252-6652
www.wildmustangs.com

Front Range Equine Rescue
P.O. Box 8807
Pueblo, CO 81008
www.wildhorserescue.org

Mustang Heritage Foundation
P.O. Box 703
Bertram, Texas 78605
512-355-3225
www.mustangheritagefoundation.org

Photo by Lisa Crosby

The author, Lisa Holderby, with Soleil.